# The Three Billy Goats GRUFF

Retold by Ellen Rudin • Illustrated by Lilian Obligado

## A GOLDEN BOOK · NEW YORK
Western Publishing Company, Inc., Racine, Wisconsin 53404

Text copyright © 1982 by Western Publishing Company, Inc. Illustrations copyright © 1982 by Lilian Obligado. All rights reserved. Printed in the U.S.A. No part of this book may be reproduced or copied in any form without written permission from the publisher. GOLDEN®, GOLDEN & DESIGN®, A FIRST LITTLE GOLDEN BOOK®, FIRST LITTLE GOLDEN BOOK® , LITTLE GOLDEN BOOKS®, and A GOLDEN BOOK® are trademarks of Western Publishing Company, Inc. Library of Congress Catalog Card Number: 81-83362 ISBN 0-307-10117-7 ISBN 0-307-68117-3 (lib. bdg.)
LMNOPQRST

Once upon a time there were three Billy Goats Gruff who lived on a hillside next to a wide, deep stream.

On the other side of the stream
was a big field of sweet, green grass.

Every day the three Billy Goats Gruff looked hungrily at the field on the other side of the stream. Every day they longed to eat some of the sweet, green grass.

But to get to the other side of the stream, they had to cross a wooden bridge. And under the bridge lived a horrible, mean troll.

One day the littlest Billy Goat Gruff said, "I cannot wait any longer. I am going to cross the bridge and eat the sweet, green grass."

"We will come, too," said his brothers. "We will be right behind you."

Little Billy Goat Gruff started across the
bridge. *Trip-trap, trip-trap* went his little hoofs
on the planks of wood.

"Who is that *trip-trapping* over my bridge?"
said the troll.

"It is I, Little Billy Goat Gruff," said Little Billy Goat Gruff in his wee, small voice.

"I am coming up to eat you!" roared the troll.

Little Billy Goat Gruff was afraid. "Oh, please don't eat me," he said. "Wait for my big brother. He is much larger and tastier than I am."

"Very well," said the troll, licking his lips. "You may go ahead."

So Little Billy Goat Gruff crossed the bridge safely and got to the field on the other side.

Then Middle Billy Goat Gruff started across the bridge. *Trip-trap, trip-trap* went his middle-sized hoofs on the planks of wood.

"Who is that *trip-trapping* over my bridge?" called the troll.

"It is I, Middle Billy Goat Gruff," said Middle Billy Goat Gruff in his middle-sized voice.

"I am coming up to eat you!" roared the troll.

Middle Billy Goat Gruff was afraid. "Please don't eat me," he said. "Wait for my big brother. He is much larger and tastier than I."

"Very well," said the troll, thinking of the
fine meal he would have. "You may go ahead."
So Middle Billy Goat Gruff crossed the bridge
safely and got to the field on the other side.

Then Big Billy Goat Gruff started across the
bridge. *TRIP-TRAP, TRIP-TRAP* went his big
hoofs on the planks of wood. The whole bridge
shook with his weight.

"Who is that *TRIP-TRAPPING* over my bridge?" roared the troll in his loudest voice.

"It is I, Big Billy Goat Gruff," shouted Big Billy Goat Gruff in *his* loudest voice.

"I suppose you are going to tell me to wait for your big brother," said the troll.

"Oh, no," said Big Billy Goat Gruff. "I am the biggest one there is."

"Then I am coming up
to eat you!" the troll shouted.
And he climbed onto the bridge.
  Big Billy Goat Gruff was not afraid.
  "I would like to see you try!" he said.

He rushed at the troll and butted him with his horns. The troll fell off the bridge and disappeared, leaving no trace.

After that the three Billy Goats Gruff crossed the bridge whenever they liked and ate their fill of sweet, green grass.

And the horrible, mean troll never bothered them again.